For my family.
–**Natasha Yim**

To Mom, Dad, and my family. Thank you for the best
Lunar New Years a girl can ever have.
–**Sophie Li**

Printed in the United States of America
First Hardcover Edition, October 2018   10 9 8 7 6 5 4 3 2
ISBN 978-1-368-02326-9
FAC-034274-19100
Library of Congress Control Number: 2018939972
For more Disney Press fun, visit www.disneybooks.com
Designed by Maureen Mulligan
Special thanks to Caroline Egan, David Lin, and Flora Zhao

DISNEY
PRINCESS

Mulan's Lunar New Year

Written by
Natasha Yim

Illustrated by
Sophie Li

DISNEY PRESS
Los Angeles • New York

It's the day before Lunar New Year, Mulan's favorite festival, and the Fa household is hustling and bustling with activity.

Mulan **leaps** out of bed,
but her legs get tangled up in the quilt,
and she lands on the floor
with a
thud.

This is not *a lucky start to the New Year,* she thinks.

She quickly untangles herself and hurries to her wardrobe. Now that Mulan is seven years old, she can finally help with the preparations!

Grandmother Fa walks into Mulan's room and says with a laugh,
"I like your originality."
   Mulan blushes as she notices that she's put her clothes on backward.

"I think you might need some **extra luck** today," Grandmother says, smiling.

"Everything you do during the **New Year festival** brings you good luck— or not. So, here's a little red for luck, eh?" she says as she places a sprig of flowers behind Mulan's ear.

After readjusting her clothes, Mulan runs into
the garden to help her mother gather flowers.

"Fresh flowers welcome the
birth of the New Year," Ma Ma
reminds her. "They bring
happiness and prosperity."

Together, they carry the flowers from the garden and place them in vases around the house. Mulan wants to sniff every bloom . . . and so does Little Brother.

CRASH!

"**Oh, no!**" Mulan cries. *This is* really *not a lucky start to the New Year.* Mulan grabs a broom and begins to sweep up the mess.

"Don't worry," Ma Ma says. "We'll sweep out the bad luck. Make sure you get all the broken pieces, though. We won't be able to sweep for a few days after the New Year starts, or we'll sweep away good luck."

"Why don't you come help me with the New Year decorations?" Father suggests when he enters the room. Mulan brightens a little. She has been learning calligraphy and is eager to show her father how well she can write.

Father hands Mulan some black paint and a paintbrush. She watches as he writes **Fu**, the Chinese character for *luck*, in perfect, bold strokes. She likes how he always ends with a fancy **twirl** of his brush.

Mulan dips her brush in black ink and carefully writes **Fu**.
She tries to end with a fancy twirl of her brush, too, but . . .

SPLAT!

Ink covers her decoration. Mulan grabs another piece of paper to try to soak up the ink, but the more she tries, the worse it gets.

Tears spring to Mulan's eyes. Her decoration is ruined!

"Ah, Mulan, no need to cry," Father says softly. "When we face a tall mountain, there's always a way through. Why don't we try again?"

So Father and Mulan
paint more **decorations**

and then hang **poems**
up around the house.

"The **Fu** is upside down, Father," she says when he hangs up her decoration. "I'll fix it."

"It's meant to be that way, Mulan," he explains.
"The upside-down **Fu** means

good luck will come to **our family**."

Mulan sighs and walks out to the garden, feeling defeated.

"Everything I do is wrong. . . .
Maybe this is just not a good luck
year for me," she says quietly.
"I wanted to be helpful, but
maybe I ruined our luck."

Mulan thinks she is alone, but Grandmother overhears her.

"Don't be sad, Mulan," she says, sitting down and taking her hand.

"Everyone makes mistakes, and luck can come in many different ways.

I have an idea! Come with me.

Maybe we'll find some luck."

Grandmother takes Mulan to the nearby street market, and they admire a dragon kite flying high in the sky. "Do you want to fly one?" Grandmother asks.

Mulan nods enthusiastically, and Grandmother buys her a beautiful kite.

"I bet you can fly yours higher," Grandmother says with a wink. But getting the kite into the air is harder than it looks.

"Oh, no! My kite!" Mulan cries.

"I think," Grandmother says, "that kite flying is a two-person job."

Together, they untangle the strings, unfurl the kite in the breeze, and watch as it floats in the sky.

"See how high it goes?" Grandmother says. "Now *that's* what I call good luck!"

As they continue traveling through the market, they spot some lanterns.

Mulan picks a **round** lantern for Grandmother,

a **square** one for her father,

and one with **tassels** for her mother.

Mulan likes the animal-shaped ones best, though,
and for herself she chooses her favorite—a dragon.

Dragons are a symbol of power and good luck, and
Mulan still thinks she needs all the luck she can get.

"It's time to go home and prepare our **New Year's Eve feast** now, Mulan," Grandmother says.

"Can I help make the dumplings?" asks Mulan.

"Of course," replies Grandmother. "I'll show you how to fold them up."

The Fa family steams fluffy white buns for happiness and reunion, makes dumplings for prosperity, and cooks noodles for long life.

"I think we're finally ready for the feast, right?" asks Mulan. "Not quite," says Ma Ma. "First, we must pay our respects to the Ancestors."

Mulan helps her parents gather the food offerings for the Ancestors.
"Now the Ancestors can celebrate Lunar New Year, too," her father says.
On the way to the temple, Mulan accidentally drops one of the buns.
"I'm sorry, Father. Will the Ancestors be angry with me?
Will this bring **more** bad luck?"

"No harm done," he reassures her.
"The Ancestors will never know."

"Well, it's about time!" cries one of the Ancestors happily.
"I hope the chicken isn't undercooked," another jokes.
"That incense smells good. I think it's lavender."
"Lunar New Year is the best!"

"Come, Mulan, it's our turn to eat," Grandmother says as they all sit down to enjoy a delicious New Year feast. "And it's a good thing, too. I'm starving!" she says with a laugh.

After dinner, Mulan heads to bed, dreaming of what Lunar New Year will bring and hoping her luck will turn.

On New Year morning, Mulan wakes up and discovers a special gift under her pillow.

"*Xin Nian Kuai Le*, Father!" says Mulan. **"Happy New Year!"**

"*Xin Nian Kuai Le*, Mulan!" says Father. "May the New Year bring you great joy and happiness!"

Mulan looks out her window and sees that the Lunar New Year parade has begun!

She runs out to watch the procession with Grandmother, Father, and Ma Ma following close behind her. In her rush to get to the parade, she trips over her skirt and falls down.

"Are you okay, Mulan?" Ma Ma asks, helping her up.

Can my luck get any worse? Mulan wonders.

Father quickly picks Mulan up and places her on his shoulders. "Now you've got the best view in the house."

Mulan smiles all the way to the parade.

Boom-be-boom!
Boom-be-boom!

Clang!
Clang!
Clang!

As they walk farther, though, Mulan has to cover her ears.
"Loud noises scare away evil spirits and the Nian, the fairy-tale beast that lives high in the mountains," says her father, comforting Mulan. "The beast is said to come down once a year to attack the villagers."

"Look, Mulan!" Ma Ma exclaims. "It's time for the dragon dance." They cheer and clap as the dragon writhes past them.

"The longer a dragon dances, the more good luck it brings," Ma Ma tells Mulan.

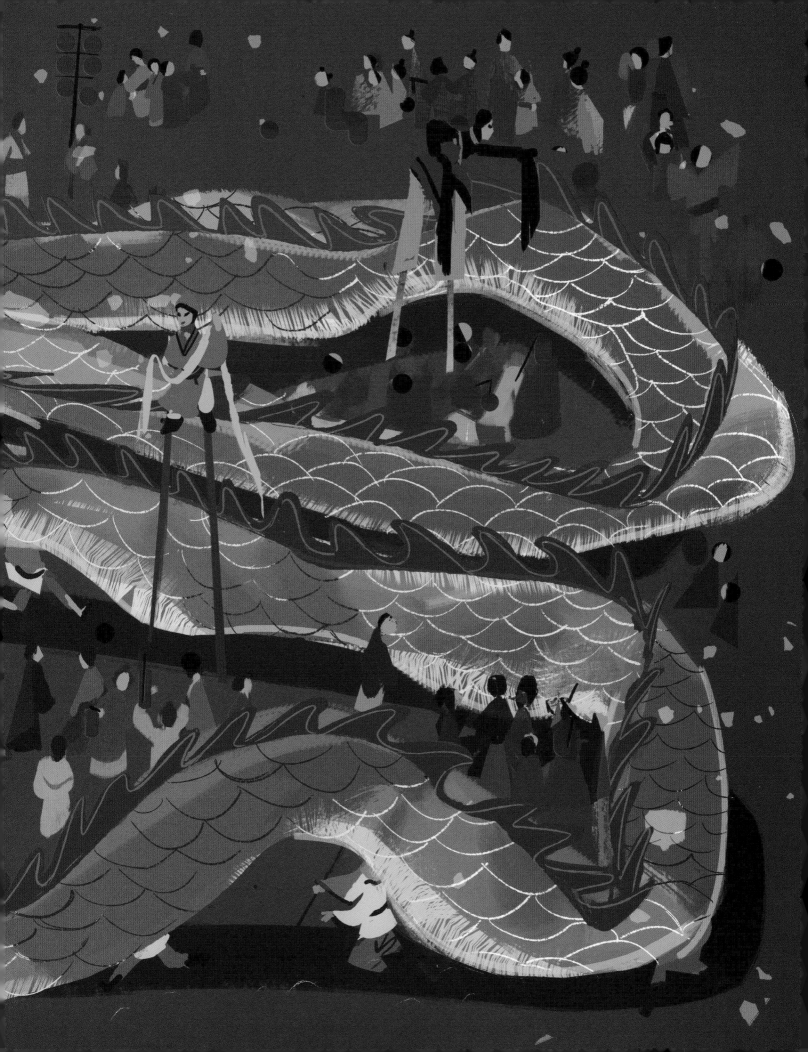

"**I do love Lunar New Year**," Mulan says. "Lighting the firecrackers, watching the parade with you . . ."
"Not such **bad luck** after all?" Grandmother Fa asks.

"I think," Mulan says, "good luck is having my **family** to share **Lunar New Year** with."

—the 結束 end—